ROGER AND THE ROTTENTROLLS
IN
REIGNING SHEEP AND TROLLS

Roger and the Rottentrolls
in
Reigning Sheep and Trolls

Written by Graham Marks
Illustrations by Gordon Firth

Based on the TV series by Tim Firth

MADCAP

First published in Great Britain in 1998 by
Madcap Books, André Deutsch Ltd
76 Dean Street, London, W1V 5HA

André Deutsch is a subsidiary of VCI plc

Based on the scripts of the TV series,
Roger and the Rottentrolls, written by
Tim Firth and produced by The Children's Company

A catalogue record for this book is available from the
British Library

ISBN 0 233 99241 3

Printed in Great Britain

CHAPTER ONE

The first thing I'd like to say is thank you for buying this book. It's an excellent choice and you're obviously a very clever sort of person for choosing this one rather than something else.

Secondly, I'd like to introduce myself: I'm your narrator. I'm like one of those voice-over chaps on the TV, here to explain bits you might not understand because you can't see the pictures (as you've probably already noticed, this isn't a comic). Not much of a job, but frankly I'm just happy to have one.

Anyway, on with the story, which is about Roger Becket and the rather strange thing that happened to him one day because of a sheep –

1

and no ordinary sheep, as Roger was about to find out.

Yes, our hero Roger. He's 10½ (well, actually he's 10¾) and he's out on his mountain bike (sorry, it's *not* a mountain bike, it's a Road Wizard with Slipstream AirMaster sports wheels and a saddle that looks like a liquorice ice lolly. Very smart, Roger).

So, there he was, out on his bike with the fancy wheels when he saw a sight to gladden the heart of any 10¾ year-old bloke on the first day of the holidays: a long, steep, come-on-what-are-you-waiting-for, raz-down-me-at-90-miles-per-hour road – and it was right in front of him.

Roger did what anyone in his position would have done. Disengaged brain, checked helmet and with an almighty push he was off! By 50 metres Roger was already going faster than his stepdad drove when his mum was in the car ... by a 100 metres he was going faster than his stepdad drove when his mum *wasn't* in the car and he was trying to get to the chip shop before it shut ...

Now, you haven't forgotten that sheep, have you? Well, it had moved into the thick bracken by the side of the road that Roger was whizzing down. It was moving quite slowly, well quite slowly compared to Roger, who was now going faster than his stepdad when he was showing off his new car on the motorway. Which, let me tell you, is dead fast for a bike, even a flash mountain bike.

Roger, who was screaming like a 100 decibel siren, never heard the odd sheepish cry of 'Jimjam YaHa!' that came from the bracken. Roger carried on screaming, but now it wasn't because he was going down the road fast enough to mean that, if he'd had wings, he'd be flying; he was screaming now because he *was* flying – off the road and into the wide blue yonder . . .

Roger wasn't on his bike any more. He was in a tree. Looking down at the ground below him.

'Oh no!' he groaned, scrambling down out of the tree. 'My Slipstream AirMaster sports wheel's bent. It's ruined now!'

Roger was just about to get really upset, as you would under the circumstances, when he noticed the signs which said things like: 'NO ENTRY!' and 'DANGEROUS VALLEY'.

'No Entry! Dangerous valley?' he repeated out loud, and looked around to see where he was.

As it turned out, Roger had fallen into a bit of the moor he'd never seen before, a bit he must have passed by loads of times. But that's 10¾ year-old boys all over – blinkered to everything but TV and football, if you ask me.

Roger read out more of the signs. 'TURN BACK! ... GO ON, HOP IT – CAN'T YOU READ THE SIGNS?'

Normally, Roger might've been scared, and I think he would have been if he'd known that two little eyes were watching him, but he was having a bad day. His arm hurt, his Slip-stream AirMaster sports wheel was now shaped like a poppadom and no one was going to tell *him* to hop it!

'Hey!' he yelled at the top of his voice. 'I'm

not scared – look, I'm in your dangerous valley! Na-na-ne-na-na!' And to finish the job off, to really show them – whoever "they" might be – what he thought of their signs, he jumped up and down to leave some foot-prints in the dirt.

'I AM ROGER, OK!' he shouted. 'ROGER WAS ERE!'

Now, that wasn't such an extraordinary thing to shout, was it? I mean he *could've* shouted something a lot more, well, boisterous . . . like 'Lancashire are rubbish at cricket!', or 'Home-work is good for you!' but he didn't. He just shouted 'Roger was ere!' and before he knew it he got leapt on by this three-foot high thing wearing a light blue cardie and a red bobble hat . . . who was also shouting 'Roger was ere!'

'Yeurgh! Get it off me!' said Roger, trying to get rid of the thing that seemed to be hugging him. After all, hugging isn't a very 'boy' thing.

'You've come!' said the thing excitedly. 'We knew you would!'

'Who are you?' asked Roger, once he'd been un-hugged.

'My name's Yockenthwaite and I'm one of the Rottentrolls,' said the thing called Yockenthwaite, 'and your name's ... *Roger Wasere* ... so that means *you* are *our* king!'

'Pardon?' said Roger.

'Pardon?' is probably what most people would say if they were told they were someone's king. Queen Elizabeth II probably said something similar when she found out she was going to be the Queen, although it's not likely some little three-foot high character wearing Oxfam rejects was the one to tell her.

'Wow!' said Yockenthwaite, dancing round Roger. 'I've found King Roger!'

'Look,' said Roger, 'I'm not *King* Roger, I'm just Roger Becket from Cowgill – there must be some mistake!'

'Don't say that, King Roger!'

'Why?'

'Cos I never do anything right, you see, King Roger,' explained Yockenthwaite. 'The others all think I'm a berk ... they sent me to the bottom of the valley for breaking the Great Ceremonial Drum of the Rottentrolls ...'

'How did you do that?' interrupted Roger.

'I was seeing if it would work as a Great Ceremonial Trampoline,' explained Yockenthwaite.

'Did it?'

'Not really ...'

Now, imagine you're Roger, standing in a hidden valley, talking to this little chap who says he's called Yockenthwaite, and he's apparently a pretty stupid example of something called a Rottentroll. How would you feel? A bit weird, right? Well it all got a whole lot more weird because ...

'Yockenthwaite!' said a voice somewhere behind Roger.

From out of nowhere came Aysgarth, undoubtedly the most important of the Rottentrolls. Yockenthwaite, we *never* bring humans into Troller's Ghyll!' he wailed. 'What's the point of putting up all them signs and ...'

'It's not a human,' beamed Yockenthwaite.

'It's Roger Wasere – I heard him shout it!'

'Just steady on a minute. Let's not jump to conclusions,' said Aysgarth. 'The *real* Roger Wasere would also be able to answer the Great Magic Riddle of the Rottentrolls,' said Aysgarth. 'What has four legs, is covered in wool and goes "B-aaaaa"!'

'What, you mean a sheep?' said Roger without thinking. I mean, even his goldfish would know the answer to that one!

'It is he!' exclaimed Aysgarth loudly. 'He is come – oh happy day!'

Aysgarth and Yockenthwaite took Roger off to one of the many caves in Troller's Ghyll, and for some reason best known to himself ('cos I certainly can't work out why he did it) he simply toddled off with them. If you ask me, I think these stories just get made up as they go along, but then us narrators aren't paid to think. We're just supposed to read what's put in front of us.

Anyway, inside the cave, which, luckily, was big enough for Roger to stand up in, they all sat down. It was a dark and gloomy place, Rottentrolls not having discovered electricity ... well, let's face it, they hadn't even discovered *tables*, let alone lights you could turn on and off, so they were all sitting round an old door they'd found dumped by the side of the road. The Rottentrolls didn't know it was a door, of course, because they're not something your bog standard cave comes supplied with, as a rule. Chairs were a bit beyond them as well and Roger found himself parked on a tatty dressing table, looking up at the stalactites growing out of the ceiling and wondering where all the crumbs on the floor came from. It was a bit like being in a coal hole after there'd been a biscuit fight, but not quite as comfortable.

'Many years ago,' began Aysgarth, once he'd settled, 'the great magician Merlin was attempting to make a royal ski resort for King Arthur when, by mistake, he picked up a crowd of Norwegian trolls in a snow cloud. As they fell out of the sky into this valley, our ancestors heard Merlin say only one thing.'

'What was that?' asked Roger.

'"Those rotten trolls have messed it all up!"' replied Aysgarth. 'Ever since, knowing our true name to be Rottentrolls, we've

waited for the great ruler of the valley –
whose name we found mystically carved in
this stone – to arrive.'

Roger looked at the stone which Aysgarth
was tapping with his cane. In it were
scratched the words, 'ROGER WAS ERE'.
'But that was just some bloke who hacked his
name in a rock!' he said.

'We must organise a crown for the coronation!' said Aysgarth, ignoring Roger.

'What's a crown?' asked Yockenthwaite.

'It's what you put on a king's head!'
scowled Aysgarth. 'Metal thing, bright
colours . . .'

'I've got one of them in me cave!' said

Yockenthwaite.

'Get off!' mocked Aysgarth.

'I 'ave – I'll get it, I'll get it!' Yockenthwaite bounced up and down. 'Can I take King Roger with me? Can I? Can I?'

'Oh, all right!' said Aysgarth, it often being easier to let Yockenthwaite have his way and then clear the mess up afterwards.

Not much later, Roger found himself sitting in another cave. He was wearing a tin can with some flowers stuck in it. Nice, if you liked that kind of thing, but . . .

'You haven't *really* got a crown, have you?' asked Roger.

'No.'

'Well, why did you say you had?'

'I wanted you to be me friend,' sighed Yockenthwaite.

'You don't have to lie to make me your friend!' said Roger, and then stopped. What am I saying – he's a three-foot high troll! 'Look, I've got to get home for my tea . . .'

But before he could do that, something else happened.

CHAPTER TWO

The something else was another Rottentroll,
and what happened was that Roger stepped
on it – I mean her.

'You've got to learn to look down when you're in Troller's Ghyll, King Roger,' said Penyghent (the cleverest of the Rottentrolls).

'That's Penyghent, Aysgarth's daughter,' explained Yockenthwaite. She's dead clever, she is – she can name eight different kinds of fish!'

'Why has he got a tin can on his head?' enquired Penyghent intelligently.

'I told your dad I'd got a crown . . .'

'Well that's not going to do, is it?' said Penyghent. 'I don't know. *Men!* Come on King Roger, let's go and find you a *real* crown.'

Outside his cave, Yockenthwaite had another go. 'How about this?' he said, waving something woolly in the air.

'You can't crown a king with a bobble hat,' said Penyghent dismissively.

'Well *I* think it looks pretty cool!'

'That just about says it all, dun't it,' said Penyghent as she took Roger off down the valley in search of something to crown him with.

Now the valley of the Rottentrolls was either one of nature's great works of art, or a complete cock-up. It all depends on your point of view. I quite like it, myself, because I hate gardening and it looks like the kind of place you don't have to do much to. By which I mean there were no lawns to mow (the sheep sort of looked after that bit – but more about them in a minute), no weeds to dig up (because just about everything was a weed, so if you dug them up there'd be nothing much left) and there were rocks everywhere. And I do mean everywhere. It looked like someone had had a fairly gigantic rock party and no one had bothered to clear up afterwards. As I say, a pretty wild place, as places go, and an ideal place to live if your two favourite colours are green and grey – which, luckily for the Rottentrolls, they are. Anyway, Penyghent, Roger and Yockenthwaite hadn't gone very far when . . .

'Alt! Oo goes there!' A sheep wearing a khaki, military-style Balaclava (horns akimbo) leapt out of a bush in front of them and barred their way.

'It's all right, Commander Harris,' said Penyghent, 'It's just us . . . and this is Roger Wasere, our new King!'

'King? I should cocoa!' said the Commander. 'Roger, King Roger – at your service, Commander Harris, head of the Troller's Ghyll SAS.'

'Special Air Service?' asked Roger.

'No! Silently Armed Sheep – all these boys, mustard-keen soldiers, ready for action!' Commander Harris nodded proudly at the field behind him.

Roger looked, but all he saw was a field full of grass-eating machines. 'He's bananas,' he muttered.

'No he's not,' whispered Yockenthwaite.

'All of them trained in the ancient martial art of Jimjam YaHA!' said the Commander.

'What's Jimjam YaHA!' asked Roger.

'Combat without contact! Fantastic thing, never fails,' Commander Harris explained. 'Only this morning I was out practising by the road over the Endless Moor when – Jimjam YaHA! – knocked some kid clean off his bike.'

'Hold on – that was me!' said Roger.

'Told you he wasn't bananas,' whispered Yockenthwaite.

Clever though she was, Penyghent wasn't able to find a crown for Roger either, and so Aysgarth had to call an Extraordinary General Meeting in the Great Cave. Actually, as meetings go it was generally not very extraordinary at all.

'Right,' said Aysgarth, 'in view of our total failure to find a crown for King Roger, it is now sadly necessary to summon Trucklecrag – the great, but slightly disappointing magician of the Rottentrolls.'

'Why's he disappointing?' asked Roger.

Before anyone could answer, Trucklecrag shuffled into the cave singing a song about banana trees to himself, tripped over his wand, and disappeared from view.

'Oh, I *see*,' said Roger.

'I think we should have that song as our National Anthem,' mumbled Trucklecrag, getting up. 'The one we've got is so *dull*.'

'We need you to magic up a crown,' Aysgarth told the dusty old magician, 'and I want no foul-ups this time – no cheese-graters, no toilet-roll holders, and above all *NO `DUSTBINS!!* – I've had it with you making dustbins all the time.'

'No problem,' said Trucklecrag, searching through his book for a crown-type spell.

'The trouble is,' Penyghent told Roger, 'that book ... it came over in the cloud from Norway!'

'So?'

'It's all in Norwegian. We can't read it.'

'Der-flurrdi-blurrder!' said Trucklecrag, waving his arms about.

'Duck!' cried Aysgarth.

Everyone ducked, there was a bang, some smoke and ... no crown.

'Where's the crown, Trucklecrag?' demanded Aysgarth.

'I don't know,' he replied.

'The valley's full of ... er ... dustbins, though!' grinned Yockenthwaite.

Aysgarth's bottom lip began to tremble. He'd been in charge of the valley for over 300 years and the day the King of the Rottentrolls had turned up he couldn't even organise a coronation. He was so frustrated he burst into tears.

'Look, look, look, never mind. We can still

have the coronation, if you want,' said Roger, trying to make him feel better.

'There's no crown!' wailed Aysgarth, 'and we can't sing the National Anthem because that *berk* Yockenthwaite tried to use the Great Ceremonial Drum as a trampoline.'

'It's all right,' grinned Roger, 'I think I've thought of something!'

What Roger had thought of was what you might call recycling. They'd been taught it at school and Roger had insisted they do some at home; all the vegetable peelings went on to the compost heap he'd started (even though his Mum and stepdad weren't what you'd call keen on horticulture) and there was a huge pile of newspapers, empty bottles and old tin cans waiting to be taken to the re-

cycling bins in the supermarket car park.

'You're messing up *our* environment, trying to help clean up everyone else's!' his Mum always complained.

Anyway, back to the story, as we narrators say.

Roger's fantastic idea was to use the torn and broken Great Ceremonial Drum as a crown. Actually, it looked rather good and the Rottentrolls thought it was great, just the kind of thing their King should wear at his coronation.

'And with this great new crown,' said Aysgarth proudly, 'I name you Roger, King of the Rottentrolls!'

The Great Cave was full to bursting with a mad selection of the Rottentrolls who all started cheering and clapping.

'And now,' continued Aysgarth, 'the singing of the Rottentrolls National Anthem – places please . . . one, two, a-one, two, three, four!' The band struck up – all playing on the (recycled) dustbins that Trucklecrag's appalling magic had filled the valley with – and the singing began:

'The proudest troll is a Rottentroll,
The noblest trolls are all the Rottentrolls,
Oh the cleverest troll is a Rottentroll –

And they're terribly modest as well!
Oh, yes we're skilful and handsome . . .'

Roger hummed along, mainly because he didn't know the words, and as the cave echoed to the sound of raucous singing, Penyghent came over to him.

'Now this is what I call a National Anthem!' she shouted. 'I didn't know dustbins could be used as instruments.'

'It's called a steel band,' explained Roger.

'You know, King Roger,' said Penyghent, 'I think you're going to make a very good King of the Rottentrolls!'

And so it was that Roger ended his first day as King of the Rottentrolls. He'd bent his bike wheel, but then, on the plus side, he'd invented the first Rottentroll steel band . . . and, with practice, they were bound to get better.

On the other hand, there were now an awful lot of dustbin *lids* to find homes for, although one had been put to good use as a new front wheel for the Road Wizard. Not quite as stylish as a Slipstream AirMaster sports wheel, but it was the only way Roger was going to get home. As he pedalled slowly up the hill (dustbin lids not really being built for speed) the big question going through his mind was – should he go back tomorrow?

'Course I'm not going back,' he decided, 'they're all completely mad!'

Oh yeah ... that's what everybody who's just been made a king by a bunch of reject garden gnomes says! You'll be back, Roger, you mark my words – think of the power! Think of the glory! Think of all the garlic pasties ... well, maybe you'd better forget about the garlic pasties, but the power and the glory bit should be pretty tempting, I'll bet.

CHAPTER THREE

The very next day, Roger was back in the hidden valley full of slightly mad rocks that was home to the Rottentrolls. Being a king, even if it is the king of a bunch of three-foot high nutters who've fallen out of a cloud, is better than just being a schoolboy, any day of the week. Especially if it's a week when you're on holiday.

In his head, Roger was having an argument with himself, as you do, and it was about him saying he'd *never* go back to be King of the Rottentrolls, and he was having the argument as he stood in the hidden valley . . .

'I'm *not* coming back to be their King – they're all completely mad!' Roger muttered. 'I was just passing and I thought I'd check to see if they were all right . . .'

'You rotten fibber!' said a little voice in his head.

'I'm not!'

'Are!'

'Not!'

'Are!'

'OK, watch this,' said Roger, fed up of arguing with himself. '*Yockenthwaite!*'

Out of a nearby bush popped Yockenthwaite.

'It's only me,' said Roger. 'I was just passing – is everything all right?'

'No!' wailed Yockenthwaite.

'Oh, well, I'll be off then!' said Roger, and

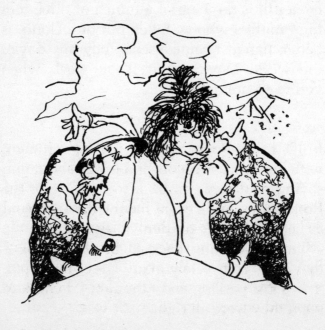

then stopped going off. 'What d'you mean, "no"?'

'You've got to help!' pleaded Yockenthwaite. 'There's invaders in the valley!' Yockenthwaite hauled Roger off to where Aysgarth and Penyghent were hiding behind a rock, clearly in a bit of a state . . .

'It arrived in the night,' said Aysgarth, pointing over the rock. 'It's a hideous monster – oh, terrible, terrible day!'

'Aysgarth, that's not a monster – that's a tent,' explained Roger.

'Just because someone's three feet high doesn't mean he's stupid,' blustered Aysgarth.

'Yo-o!' said Yockenthwaite.

'Except in his case . . .' sighed Aysgarth.

'The monster's *inside* the tent,' said Penyghent.

'What, you mean that tent's eaten a monster?' said Yockenthwaite.

'Oh, will you shut up!' Aysgarth said, batting the bobble on Yockenthwaite's bobble hat.

'And every so often, King Roger,' said Penyghent, 'whaever's inside does this . . .' As they watched, loud burping sounds echoed round the valley, and out of the tent flew a couple of empty drink cans. They joined empty tins of beans, plastic bottles of pop and enough waste paper to make a life-sized *papier maché* sculpture of Arnold Schwarzenegger.

'There aren't any monsters in there,' explained Roger. 'Just two humans *behaving* like monsters. Don't worry, I'll deal with this.' He strode purposefully over to the tent and knocked on it. Then it occurred to him that knocking on canvas was about as useful as trying to nail down water, so he just sort of coughed instead.

'What d'you want, *kid*?' said the first bloke to stick his head out.

'Yeah, *kid*, what d'you want?' said the second bloke.

'Sorry,' said Roger, nervously, 'but this is a private valley – you can't camp here.'

'What a King!' said Aysgarth, from behind the rock.

'What a hero!' sighed Penyghent.

'What a nice tent,' said Yockenthwaite.

'Listen, kid,' said the first bloke, 'we can camp anywhere we want to – and d'you know why? Tell him, Devvo!'

'Our mums are members of the National Trust!' said Devvo. 'Right, Mook?'

'No!' said Mook. 'It's because we're *tuff*!'

Roger swallowed so hard that people heard it in Cowgill's main street.

'You can't throw litter about either,' he said, trying another angle.

'Course we can, it's easy – look,' said Mook, chucking some more rubbish out of the tent.

Roger put on his sternest look. 'I'm telling you to stop!'

'You think we're scared of you, kid?' asked Mook.

Roger remembered his stepdad saying that, whenever a bully says 'D'you think I'm scared of you?' it usually means that he really is . . .

'Yes!' said Roger, testing out his stepdad's theory. This was a brave, but silly thing to do, under the circumstances, because Mook and

Devvo had never heard of Roger's stepdad's theory and proceeded to duff him up good and proper. Which just goes to show how dangerous it can be trying to prove other people's ideas.

CHAPTER FOUR

'So,' said Aysgarth, 'they weren't scared of you then?'

As Roger's stepdad had got it all wrong on this occasion, Roger now looked like he'd been in a fight with a very full bin bag. Which, as it happens, wasn't so very far from the truth.

'Have a towel, King Roger,' said Penyghent.

'Right!' snarled Roger, 'that is it. I'm just not having this – if *I* don't scare them off, there must be *something* in this valley that will . . . something scary that's really, really . . !'

'There *is* something scary in Troller's Ghyll, King Roger,' said Aysgarth, his voice trembling at the very thought of what he was thinking about, 'but it's *much* too scary to talk about.'

'Not *in* it,' whispered Penyghent, '*under* it.'

'So what is it?' asked Roger.

'It's called the Barguest,' explained Penyghent. 'It's a huge, hairy doggy thing, with eyes as big as dinner plates! It lives in the disused lead mines underneath the valley, and every full moon . . .'

'Don't!' pleaded Aysgarth.

'. . . it comes out of its lair,' Penyghent ignored her dad, 'and stalks down the Ghyll . . .'

'*Don't!*' cried Aysgarth.

'. . . and all we can see are the two red lights of its eyes going round in the darkness,' Penyghent's voice had now risen almost to a scream, 'with this terrible noise – *WAAA-AAAAAHH*!!'

'STOP TALKING ABOUT IT!!!' yelled Aysgarth. 'Stop talking about the Barguest this minute, Penyghent. This isn't getting us anywhere – summon up all Rottentrolls to the Great Cave; we need a brain-storming session.'

The trouble with Rottentrolls having a brain-storming session is that, by and large, they don't have brains. So the meeting was less of a brain-*storm*, and more of a brain-*slight gust of wind*.

'I know!' said Askrigg, the most sporty of the Rottentrolls. 'Let's have a game of American foot-ball!'

'How's that going to scare anyone away?' asked Penyghent, who knew a stupid suggestion when she heard one.

'Ah . . .' pondered Askrigg, 'it won't, prob-ably. But it's a great game . . . hup, two quarterback, line out – hup, hup, hup!'

'Askrigg, shut up, will you,' said Aysgarth.

31

'And take that ridiculous hat off!'

'I like it,' muttered Askrigg, stroking the shiny helmet he was wearing. 'I like it better than me 'ead.'

They all umm'd and ahh'd as they tried to think of *something* scary that would rid the valley of the ghastly, rubbish-strewing invaders in their garish orange tent. It was really hard work, but someone had to do it. After quite a long time, Kettlewell, the dangerous chef of the Rottentrolls, barged into the Great Cave shouting: 'Dinner!' as she chucked a dish on the table. 'Right,' she said,

'I've baked you all some . . .'

'Garlic pasties,' groaned the assembled company, 'Boring . . .'

'Who said that?' roared Kettlewell, eyes bulging like marshmallows as she shook her kitchen trowel in the air. Garlic pasties were what she did best . . . in fact they were all she *ever* did.

'Oh, they're very nice, Kettlewell,' said Aysgarth.

'Who said "Boring"? I'll deck yer!'

'Kettlewell, they're really very, *very* nice,' said Aysgarth, soothingly. 'It's just some-times, possibly, it might be fun to have some-thing like . . . I don't know . . . like honey flapjacks. You know, once in a while.'

'I don't do honey flapjacks, I just do garlic pasties!'

'We know,' someone mumbled.

'Who said that!'

'Stop it!' said Roger, looking down on the arguing Rottentrolls from his throne. 'We're supposed to be fighting the invaders, not each other!'

'I tell you what,' mumbled Trucklecrag, 'I could magic you up a few scary rabbits . . . I can do rabbits, I've got rabbits sussed, me. Watch this – *Flurr-ecky-eckle-ek-benny'n'bjorn!*'

'Duck!' cried Penyghent.

'Ooh . . . will you look at that!' said

33

Trucklecrag, pointing at what he'd magicked up. 'What a fantastic rabbit . . . all silver and square!'

'It's a toaster,' said Roger.

'A toaster? Is it? Oh pig,' mumbled Trucklecrag, 'I thought it was a new type of rabbit.'

'I could throw the toaster at them,' suggested Askrigg, 'you know, like in American football.'

Aysgarth perked up. 'Now *there's* an idea!' he said. 'We could throw things and make them two louts think the sky was falling in!'

'How about using these garlic pasties?' asked Yockenthwaite.

'Who said that?' growled Kettlewell.

'Come on, Yockenthwaite,' said Roger, taking a pasty, 'Kettlewell's gone to a lot of trouble to bake these – we can't use them as *missiles*!'

I should just point out that Roger said this *before* he'd eaten one of Kettlewell's efforts, which only goes to prove that old Rottentroll saying: 'Never judge a pasty until you've put it in your mouth.'

'On second thoughts . . .' mumbled Roger,

wondering if it was OK for kings to spit out food that tasted like garlic-flavoured cement (and stuck to the roof of your mouth like, well, cement, really).

Even Kettlewell had to admit that, as ammunition went, her garlic pasties were pretty darn lethal, so she didn't make much of a fuss over them being used to bombard the bright orange tent and its inhabitants.

Roger led the way and directed the operation, and it was with great pride that the Rottentrolls watched a bucket-load of Kettlewell's finest creations rain down on the invaders . . .

'What was that?' said Mook, as he and Devvo heard what sounded like hail outside the tent.

Devvo poked his head out. 'Looks like a load of weird smelly rocks,' he said, bringing one back in.

'That's lucky,' grinned Mook. 'We were looking for something to hammer the tent pegs in properly!'

When safely back in the Great Cave, everyone was sitting round feeling very depressed, including Roger who had a black plastic bag

full of all the rubbish the invaders had thrown out so far.

'What a great success *that* plan was,' said Roger. 'They'll be here all week and by then the valley'll be just one big rubbish tip. Let's face it, *we* need something as scary as the Barguest . . .' It was then that Roger had a fairly decent idea. 'Hold on!' he said excitedly. 'A *Barguest* – we could use a Barguest to scare them off!'

'No! Anything but that!' cried every single Rottentroll in the Great Cave.

'Calm down, calm down. I don't mean *the* Barguest,' explained Roger, 'I mean *a* Barguest – we'll make a pretend one! It only comes out at night, so as long as what we've got has two red eyes and goes *WAAA-AAAAAHH!!* they won't know the difference!'

'But we haven't got anything to make it with,' said Penyghent.

'We have now,' grinned Roger, holding up

the bulging black plastic bag. 'Their rubbish!'

It was only as Roger explained how two tin cans (end on) with candles in, plus cherry pop bottles (cut in half) over the ends would make a couple of great pretend Barguest's eyes, that he realised how glad he was his Mum had made him watch *Blue Peter* . . .

'I can do that, King Roger!' yelled Yocken-thwaite, when Roger had finished. 'Can I make them?'

'No!' said Aysgarth firmly. 'You always mess things up.'

'I won't this time,' pleaded Yockenthwaite. 'Give me a chance – please, please, *pleeeeease!*'

It was a dark and moonless sky that night, mainly because of the thick clouds. The two scruffy invaders had gone to bed early, as there was nothing else to do. Then they heard the noise . . .

'Did you 'ear summink?' asked Mook, turning on his torch and shining it in Devvo's face.

'What?' said Devvo, turning *his* torch on and shining it in Mook's face.

'Sounded like *r-r-r-r-r-r-r*,' said Mook. 'Go and take a dekko.'

'You stick yer 'ead out,' said Devvo. 'You're

the one said 'e was tuff.'

'You're the one who agreed,' replied Mook, just as the sound got nearer the tent.

'I want me Mum!' whispered Devvo.

'Shut up, it's prob'ly nothin',' said Mook. 'Prob'ly just some furry animal, and we're not bothered by little furry animals, are we . . ?'

'No . . .'

Just then the tent was lit up by the ghostly glow of two huge red eyes. And when I say huge, I mean socking *enormous*! Really, the biggest red eyes you have ever seen. Then, whatever the eyes belonged to went, *WAAA-AAAAAHH!!* Well, that was it. Our two brave litter louts were off into the night – in their stripy wincyette pyjamas – leaving everything they'd brought with them behind.

'They've gone!' yelled Roger triumphantly, coming out from behind the rock where he and the rest of the Rottentrolls had been hiding.

'YA-HAAAAY!!' everyone cheered.

'Well done, Yockenthwaite!' beamed Aysgarth. 'For the first time in his life he's done something right! Three cheers for . . . where is he?'

Yockenthwaite was nowhere to be seen, but Roger eventually found him hiding in his cave . . .

'I messed it up, didn't I,' said Yockenthwaite miserably. 'I let everyone down.'

'Er . . .' said Roger, 'you mean that wasn't *you* out there in the valley just now?'

Yockenthwaite held up his hands. 'I got me hands stuck in the tins, King Roger,' he said. 'I couldn't make a rubbish monster . . . all *I* could make was a monster that was rubbish.'

'But Yockenthwaite . . .' Roger began very slowly, '. . . the pretend Barguest was out there a moment ago, and it scared off the invaders.' A slightly frightening thought crept up out of a small, dark bit of Roger's mind and cleared its throat . . . 'It can't have

39

been the *real* Barguest, can it?' said Roger. 'I mean, it's not a full moon tonight, is it?'

'Oh 'eck . . .' said Yockenthwaite, looking out of the cave at a big white, dappled and unmistakably full, moon.

'I think it might be better if we said it *was* you, OK?' muttered Roger.

So all the other Rottentrolls never, *ever*, knew it was the real Barguest that put the wind up the invaders. Aysgarth was so pleased he decided to throw a midnight feast in celebration, at which Yockenthwaite was the slightly embarrassed guest of honour, and they all had a feast of cherry pop and baked beans that Mook and Devvo had kindly left behind. Which goes to prove another old Rottentroll saying (actually, it's a brand-new one they just made up) which goes: 'Every orange tent full of smelly humans also has some tasty stuff in it.'

CHAPTER FIVE

With the success of the Great Battle of the Invaders behind him, Roger Becket (otherwise known as King of the Rottentrolls, at least that's what he was known as in one particular hidden valley full of slightly mad rocks and slightly madder trolls) was a pretty happy 10¾ year old. Especially as today was a sunny day in Troller's Ghyll.

The air was crisp, the sky was blue and the sun was baking. By which, I mean it was hot, rather than standing in a kitchen with an egg whisk. Anyway . . . as Roger walked into the valley he had no idea that today was more than just a lovely day. Today was *the* most special day in the Rottentroll calendar.

'All right?' said Roger, coming across Penyghent.

'Oh, King Roger,' she said, looking up from what she was doing. 'Great, you're just in time!'

'What are you doing, Penyghent?'

'Collecting blueberries,' replied Penyghent, picking something up off the ground and putting it over Roger's head. 'Terrific. The Winner's Garland I've just made fits you.'

Roger wasn't the type of chap who went in for wearing a lot of flowers, so he started to take the garland off . . .

'No,' said Penyghent, 'you keep it on, King Roger!'

'What?'

'The judge has to wear it during the day of the competition,' she explained. 'Then, at the end, he presents it to the winner!'

'Winner?'

42

'It's the Rottentroll of the Year Contest today,' said Penyghent, 'and *you're* the judge, King Roger . . .'

Penyghent took Roger (still wearing the rather fetching festoon of flowers) off to the Great Cave, where every Rottentroll in Troller's Ghyll had gathered. There was an air of expectant turmoil in the cave, which basically meant people were thinking about pushing each other about . . .

'Rottentrolls and Trollslips!' cried Penyghent. 'Welcome to the 961st Rottentroll of the Year Competition – and the first ever to be judged by our new King, Roger Wasere!'

This was followed by a burst of uncontrolled clapping, cheering and general mayhem from the crowd.

'Oh, flippin' 'eck . . .' thought Roger.

'Can we have contestant Number One, please,' announced Penyghent.

'Me! It's me!' yelled someone from the back of the Great Cave.

This was followed by a burst of uncontrolled sighs and muttered 'Oh no!'s from the crowd.

'What's the matter?' asked Roger.

'It's Sigsworthy Crags,' said Aysgarth, gloomily. 'I should disregard this competitor, King Roger.'

'Why? I think he looks great!' grinned Roger. 'He's made a brill job of colouring his hair wrong and not shaving and putting on a stupid hat to make himself look like a complete nutter.'

'Actually,' said Aysgarth, 'that's him having tidied himself up a bit for the competition.'

'You mean that's not his act?'

'Fraid not,' Aysgarth shook his head. 'His act will consist of him telling us he's built an airship and ends up with him making a noise like a dog. It always does.'

44

Pushing his way through the crowd and standing up in front of everyone, contestant Number One began his act.

'I, Sigsworthy Crags,' said Sigsworthy Crags, 'would like to recite a poem . . . It is called "The Airship I Have Built".'

'What did I tell you,' said Aysgarth.

Sigsworthy began:

'There was an inventor called Sigsworthy
    Crags,
Who built a big airship, one day in his
    CAVE!!
But no one believed him, and they'd all
    regret it,
The day he went *flying* right out of the
    valley.
Over ponds that were still, and seas that
    were rough,
And lakes that were rough and rough
that
    was ruff . . .
Ruff, ruff, ruff ra-ooooo!!'

'Here we go,' sighed Aysgarth. 'I think we've seen enough of this, Penyghent!'

'Ladeez and gentletrolls,' said Penyghent, 'Sigsworthy Crags . . .'

The next person up was Trucklecrag, the great, but slightly disappointing magician.

Roger wondered what he was going to do, and he didn't have to wait long to find out. Trucklecrag announced he was going to make Penyghent rise off the floor and float, on her back, in mid-air – whereupon she would start to spin round and speak in fluent Dutch.

Yockenthwaite leant into Roger. 'She'll turn into a pizza,' he whispered to Roger. 'He practised on me all yesterday. You just end up as a pizza.'

Surprisingly, Yockenthwaite was absolutely right (although he'd failed to mention that the pizza came in a handy cardboard box with a lid, and had a rather delicious-smelling pepperoni topping). Anyway, it took Trucklecrag twenty minutes to turn the pizza back into Penyghent, by which time it was the turn of the Nab Twins to take the stage . . .

'Who are the Nab Twins?' Roger asked Aysgarth.

'They're our two teenage Rottentrolls, I'm afraid.'

'Oh.' said Roger, who still had another 2¼ years to go before he'd be a teenager and couldn't quite see what the fuss was all about.

'They're very trendy,' said Yockenthwaite, who wished he had a baseball cap he could put on backwards like the Nab Twins.

'All right, you *grown-ups*,' sneered Great Nab, plunking a guitar he'd made out of an old corned beef tin, a thin plank of wood and some string. 'We're goin' to, like, *play* you dull old, like, *wrinklies* a song!'

As with most teenagers, the Nab Twins were a lot of mouth, far too much trousers and not enough vocabulary (like, *words*, man, nah'wo I meeen?). They stood on the stage and yelled things like 'Outrageous, dude!' and 'Radical, man!' and 'Oooh! Check out the bossy babe!'. They yelled that when Penyghent told them to get on with their act because she had a schedule to keep to.

'All right, all right!' said Small Nab, peering over his drum. 'For our entry we've, like, *written* a protest song . . . and it's called "We Protest About Having to Enter This Contest"!'

'I'm sorry about this, King Roger,' Aysgarth

apologised. 'I wonder if I went through this stage?'

Before Roger could say anything, Great Nab played a loud and completely out-of-tune chord on his DIY guitar, and the twins began to sing . . . or rather squawk.

'People try to put us down!'
'Just because we're small and round.
We can't be bothered to write a song,
So that's the end.
No it isn't.
Yes it is!
Ahahahahaha . . .'

That was that, and the Nab Twins left the stage to the sound of the odd clap echoing off the roof of the Great Cave. From then on, the competition went from mad to madder; Kettlewell gave a display of dangerously boring knitting, during which she made a mustard yellow cardigan for Roger (which went on for some time); Askrigg demonstrated his sporting skills by throwing Penyghent about, and at the very end of the contest Yockenthwaite sang his very favourite song: 'There Were Ten Thousand in the Bed . . .'

'Gerroff!!' everyone in the cave (including Roger) yelled.

'That's not fair!' said Yockenthwaite, slouching off the stage.

'So, King Roger,' said Penyghent, 'which one was the best?'

Roger didn't know what to do or say. All the competitors were completely different (except that they were also all as terrible as each other) and the last thing he wanted to do was offend anyone. What he needed to do was play for time . . .

'I need to have a bit of a think,' said Roger.

CHAPTER SIX

Roger left the Great Cave and went for a walk among the mad-shaped rocks of Troller's Ghyll, which felt like a very good place for thinking. It was a terrific clear-your-head spot ... a fantastic let's-think-rationally-there-must-be-a-way-out-of-this sort of place. As luck would have it, it was also the place where Commander Harris lived ...

'Ha-*yaaaaahh!*' hissed the Commander, creeping up behind Roger as he sat on top of one of the rocks, thinking. 'Who goes there – come no further or I shall be forced to use the ancient martial art of Jimjam YaHA!'

'It's me, Commander,' said Roger.

'Oh ho! Roger, King Roger, I should cocoa!' said the Commander. 'What're you doing up here?'

'Thinking about something,' replied Roger. 'I've got a very important decision to make.'

'Ah yes! Important decisions,' the Commander nodded sagely. 'Do a lot of them meself, what with being head of the Troller's Ghyll SAS – ha*yaaah!*'

'What exactly is Jimjam YaHA, Commander Harris?'

'Jimjam YaHA? Ancient form of combat I picked up in the jungle,' said the Commander, proudly waving his front legs about. 'I used to be an Army mascot, y'see.'

'How does it work?'

'See that bloke on the bike over there?' the Commander pointed out over the moor. 'Aaaaah-*aaaaah!* Jimjam YaHA!' Up until that point, Roger had thought Commander Harris was probably a few slices short of a full loaf, but as he watched the cyclist he was amazed to see him fly right off his bike into the bracken.

'That's amazing!' said Roger.

'I should cocoa,' huffed the Commander. 'Fancy a cup of tea in me command hut?'

From the outside, the Commander's hut looked like the kind of shed normally found mouldering on an allotment, but inside it was a different story. Inside it was stuffed to bursting with electronic surveillance equipment and lit by the sickly glow of radar screens. Roger was impressed.

'What does all this do?' he asked.

'Keeps an eye on me troops, all the sheep in the Ghyll,' said the Commander proudly. 'Every move they make gets picked up by the scanners!'

'What are they doing now?' Roger peered at the screens, but couldn't make any sense of what he saw.

'Er . . . eating grass, mainly – except Bob, who's hang-gliding off a telegraph pole in . . .' The Commander peered more closely. 'Oh no, actually he's eating grass now as well.'

'What was it like in the Army, Commander Harris?' Roger asked, taking his eyes off the screens at last.

'The Army?' pondered the Commander. 'All depended on what the bloke feeding you was like, in my experience.'

'Was yours any good?'

'Mine? The best, me boy!' said the Commander. 'Private Jimmy MacCreedy, bally hero!'

'A hero?' said Roger. 'With medals?'

'Not a one. Never had any medals,' frowned the Commander. 'Never got promoted nor nothing ... but to *me* he was a hero; fed me, cleaned me, de-loused me, and in the middle of the jungle he found fresh grass for me. And no one knew he did all that.'

'No one?' asked Roger.

If this was a movie, now would be the moment where the chap with the violin would start to sound like he was strangling a cat, which would bring tears to your eyes. In other words, the Commander got a bit soppy ...

'You see, King Roger,' he said, solemnly, 'it isn't always the people who put on the biggest shows who are the heroes. No, very often there are people who carry on quietly in the background, and no one really notices them. They can be heroes, too.'

(End of violins.)

'Commander Harris!' said Roger, 'I think you've just helped me make my important decision!'

It's amazing how good you can feel when you've finally decided to do something. You suddenly feel all happy and skip-and-jumpy and that cloud that's been following you around magically disappears. Mad, really, but there you go ... anyway, that's how Roger felt as he made his way back to the Great Cave where all the Rottentrolls were waiting to find out who'd won the Rottentroll of the Year Contest.

'Have you made your choice, King Roger?' asked Aysgarth.

'Yes,' said Roger, sitting in his throne, 'I've decided . . .'

'Oooooh!!' went the crowd.

'. . . I've decided to announce the winners in reverse order,' Roger continued. 'In third place, for his brill song "There Were Ten Thousand in the Bed" – Yockenthwaite!'

'Yo-o!' said Yockenthwaite, who'd never won anything before. 'The big Number Three!'

'And in second place, for this *tremend*ous cardigan,' Roger pointed to the huge orange

thing he was wearing, in case anyone had missed it, 'Kettlewell!' 'Right,' She said, 'fair enough.'

'Boring . . .' mumbled a few of the braver types in the crowd.

'*WHO SAID THAT!!* '

'And this year's Rottentroll of the Year is . . . ' Roger let them all wait for a second or two more, '. . . Penyghent!'

'No! No, you can't do that!' said a very surprised Penyghent. 'I'm not in it, y'see – I'm only the organiser.'

'Precisely!' grinned Roger. 'The organiser who built the stage, picked the blueberries, made the Winner's Garland, wrote the schedule, put up with being turned into a pizza and chucked about like a football. Without *you*, Penyghent, there would have been no competition at all – and *that's* why I'm making you the winner of it!'

A huge roar of cheers boomed about the Great Cave, and every one of the Rottentrolls, even those who believed *they* should have won something, thought what a fantastic king they'd got in Roger Wasere!

And that night, when Roger got back to his home in Cowgill – home to being plain Roger Becket of 32 Hugh Gaitskill Crescent – his Mum couldn't understand where on Earth he could've got such a huge mustard-coloured cardigan from. Or why, when he went to sleep later, he had this big, satisfied smile on his face – as though he'd done something really quite clever . . .

CHAPTER SEVEN

Well, here we are. Tuesday morning and who's this cycling over the endless moor towards Troller's Ghyll? Oh, *what* a surprise! It's Roger 'I'm not a King, really' Becket. The one who said he was *never* coming back because all his subjects were completely mad. I'm sure that's what he said, wasn't it? Well, there's no point in asking because kings will never have a proper argument because they can always say something like 'Shut it, will you' and walk away.

So here was Roger, back again. He cycled into the hidden valley, parked his bike behind a rock and walked off, only stopping when he was going past the cave belonging to Kettlewell, the dangerous chef of the Rottentrolls. Why, you might ask, is she dangerous? Read on . . .

'Get down and *stay* down!' Roger heard her yelling. 'Don't move, or I'll deck yer!'

Then Roger heard a lot of thumping and grunting and saw a frying pan, a trowel and an empty bag of flour come flying out of the cave as Kettlewell shouted, 'Right! Take *that* ... and *this* ... and try *this* for size!'

If it had been anyone else's cave Roger would have dashed in to stop the fight, but by now he knew it was just Kettlewell making garlic pasties.

'Mind yer 'ead!' boomed Kettlewell, as Roger came in to the cave. 'You rotten pastry – you stay flat or I'll deck yer!'

'Kettlewell,' said Roger, standing well back, 'who taught you to cook?'

'Me Dad,' she said, aiming a fierce windmill of a punch at the quivering lump on the

table in front of her. 'Hay-*yaaargh!*'

'Was he a wrestler?'

'Course he wasn't a wrestler – he were a cook!' said Kettlewell. 'It was him that taught me the great secret of how to make garlic pasties, which in turn I'll pass on to me daughter, Strid.'

'What secret's that?' enquired Roger.

'Speed,' replied Kettlewell, thumping the pastry into complete submission. 'Rottentrolls hate eating garlic pasties when they're cold, so you've got to be quick – in the oven, out the oven, run up the valley and tell 'em it's all ready. Then, back in the kitchen and get 'em on the table. Done.'

'Wouldn't it be less *dangerous* to do everything a bit more slowly?' asked Roger.

'How?'

'Find another way to tell everyone dinner's ready.'

'Find another way?' snorted Kettlewell. 'The caves are all *over* the Ghyll and I'm in here! You can't talk to people unless you go and *see* them, can yer?'

'A-*ha!*' said King Roger. 'That's where *I* might be able to help . . .'

Roger then went straight over to Yockenthwaite's cave, because, he'd discovered, if you ever wanted something, Yockenthwaite probably had it . . . somewhere. Getting out his spiffy eight-blade Swiss-style Taiwanese Army knife, his Kingship started to make something. Although, if you ask me, he shouldn't be interfering – but kings don't see it as interfering, they look at it as ruling . . .

'What d'you want all these old tin cans for?' asked Yockenthwaite.

'A-*ha*!' said King Roger. Again. 'In the world outside Troller's Ghyll,' Roger went on, 'we can talk to people who are a long way away without going to see them, because *we* have invented *this* – the telephone!'

'With respect, Your Majesty,' said Aysgarth, when he saw what Roger had made, 'it's just two tin cans joined by a bit of string.'

'A-*ha*!' said Roger, for the third time. 'Put

the tin I gave you to your ear, Aysgarth,' he
commanded.

'To me ear?' said Aysgarth, looking at what
had so very recently contained *Scrummy-
Nuggets Tuna Flavoured Cat Food*. 'If I must . . .'

'Are you ready?' asked Roger.

'For what?'

'Hello,' Roger said into his tin.

'*Waaaargh!!*' screamed Aysgarth, dropping
the can. 'He was here! It was like he was
standing right by me ear!'

The Nab Twins thought this was, like, outrageous . . . you know, really *radical*, man.

'That's how the telephone works.' Said
Roger.

Roger then went on to explain, in great detail,
how a telephone worked, but he could see
that all the Rottentrolls who'd gathered to
watch the experiment had no idea what he
was on about, so he said:

'The words go along the string, from one
can to the other . . .'

'How come they don't fall off?' said
Yockenthwaite, (the only Rottentroll stupid
enough not to mind anyone knowing how
thick he was).

'No, it's not like that,' sighed Roger, twang-

ing the connection between the two cans. 'Speaking makes the string vibrate ... go up and down, see?'

'Doesn't that make it even *more* difficult for them to stay on?' frowned Yockenthwaite. 'Do they have to wear, like, special boots?'

'Load of rubbish!' said a dark, sour voice. '*Rubbish!*'

The voice fitted the person standing at the entrance to the Great Cave perfectly. It was Blacksyke (for those of you who don't know, Blacksyke was actually Aysgarth's sister, but while *he'd* ended up all nice and friendly, *she'd* turned out all bitter and become the rottenest of the Rottentrolls). She was dressed completely in black (naturally), wearing a hat with a veil (also black).

'How does holding a tin to our ear make dinner hot?' scowled Blacksyke.

'A-*ha*!' said Roger.

I've lost count of how many times he's said it now.

'Because this,' Roger held up his tin, 'is part of our new Troller's Ghyll Extraordinary Dinner Telephone Service!'

As soon as Roger had set it up, stringing a long piece of, well, string, from Kettlewell's

cave to the Great Cave, he tested it out . . .

'The pasties are ready! The pasties are *ready*! *THE PASTIES ARE READY!!!*' Kettlewell barked into her tin.

'Wa-*hey*!!' yelled all the listening Rottentrolls.

'There you go,' grinned Roger. 'You've seen the future, and it works!'

But that wasn't the end of it, oh no. For the Extraordinary Dinner Telephone to work, everyone needed one running from *their* cave to Kettlewell's. So Roger installed them all personally . . .

'Thanks, King Roger,' said Penyghent.

'Dig the food groove, man!' gushed Great Nab.

'Yeah, like, radical nosh, King R!' agreed Small Nab.

'A phone! A phone! A-ra-*ooooo*!!' said Sigsworthy Crags.

Now, of course, Kettlewell would be run off her feet having to ring everyone up individually to say the same thing over and over . . .

'No she won't,' interrupted Roger, as you do if you're a king. 'I've thought of that!'

'*DINNER!!*' bellowed Kettlewell, into a dustbin with everyone's telephone string attached to it.

So that was how everyone in Troller's Ghyll got their pasties red-hot. The Extraordinary

Dinner Telephone was a great success, and Roger was *incredibly* pleased with himself and his wonderful new idea.

The only problem was, it – by which I mean the whole telephone thing – didn't stop there. Oh my goodness me, no . . .

CHAPTER EIGHT

The trouble with having ideas is that, even with types as brainless as the Rottentrolls, *they* start having them as well. Which, as you'll see, isn't necessarily such a good thing . . .

'Hold on!' cried Askrigg, who up till now had never had any ideas except 'Let's play some more American football!' 'If we've got Extraordinary Dinner Telephones in our caves, we could just call Kettlewell when we're hungry, come and pick up our pasties and go back to our caves. Sort of like a take-away.'

And so it was that without realising it, King Roger invented the very first Troller's Ghyll call-out pasty service. But it didn't end there. People started asking for little extras;

Aysgarth decided he liked his garlic pasties with extra parsley and salt; Great Nab wanted his easy on the garlic, with extra sunflower seeds; Yockenthwaite wanted his sunny-side up and Penyghent asked for hers with a side order of blueberries. Kettlewell was not a happy dangerous chef.

'You and your rotten telephone!' she roared. 'I've been rushed off me feet all day doing special orders – and I never see anyone for longer than a split second!' Roger looked round the empty Great Cave. 'Hold on,' he said, 'I don't want to eat on me own!'

And, of course, it didn't end there either, because one idea *always* leads to another . . .

'King Roger! King Roger! You know this ber*rilliant*, absolutely yo-o dinner telephone?' said Yockenthwaite a bit later.

'Yes?'

'Well, I found some more tin cans,' said Yockenthwaite, 'so could I have one that isn't a *dinner* telephone, just a sort of *chatty* telephone – so I could talk to Penyghent in her cave?'

'I s'pose so,' said Roger.

But of course as soon as Yockenthwaite had a chatty telephone to Penyghent's cave, he wanted one to everyone else's cave as well. And right after that everyone else wanted the same, and soon these were the sort of conversations you could hear . . .

'Hello Penyghent, Yockenthwaite here . . . so what did you do today? Stayed in your cave? Me too . . .'

'That you, Askrigg? Yes, it's me, Sigsworthy . . . no, I've just stayed in all day . . .'

'No, Dad, I've not been anywhere . . .'

Even Great Nab started to phone Small Nab . . . in the same cave. The entire length and breadth of Troller's Ghyll was covered in a tangled web of Extraordinary Chatty Telephone lines, and quite soon no one bothered coming out of their caves any more and the whole place became completely deserted.

Suddenly, King Roger wasn't so sure about his fantastic idea anymore. Suddenly he realised that being able to talk all the time meant no one was actually *meeting* anybody any more . . . and, just maybe this wasn't such a good thing.

Then he realised there was no one around to play games with, either (and fishing's a bit *dull* on your own). Finally, he had to admit that it didn't really matter *that* much if your pasty wasn't piping hot if there was never anyone around to eat it with. He decided something *had* to be done . . .

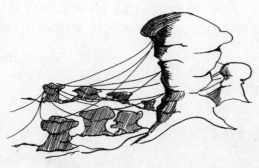

Roger raced out of the Great Cave and into the valley. He tore round and round gathering up all the string like some kind of manic candyfloss machine, ripping the tins out of all the caves as he went. The Rottentrolls were a bit surprised, I can tell you; they'd only *just* got used to being connected to phones and couldn't quite get the hang of being cut-off . . .

'What in blazes ... where's me phone!' said Aysgarth. 'I was just in the middle of telling someone I hadn't really *done* anything to talk to them about.'

'A-*ha*!' said Roger, for the last time that day. 'There's another brilliant idea we have in the world outside Troller's Ghyll for telling people when dinner's ready.'

'There is?' asked Aysgarth.

'Yes,' said Roger, 'and all it takes is this string wound up into a ball, a tin can and a dustbin!'

'And what's this invention called, King Roger?' asked a curious Aysgarth.

'An Extraordinary Dinner Bell!'

And so it was that from then on all the Rottentrolls knew when it was tea time because, wherever they were in Troller's Ghyll, when Kettlewell hit the new Extraordinary Dinner Bell they could *all* hear it. Which meant that the garlic pasties were always hot, and which also meant that King Roger learned that being a King doesn't always mean you're right, although he'd never admit that to any of the Rottentrolls.

'I mean,' he thought as he cycled home, 'who could have predicted that the Extraordinary Dinner Telephone was going to be such a bad idea?'

A-*ha* !

CHAPTER NINE

Of all the mad-shaped rocks in Troller's Ghyll, one of the maddest was the Rumblerock. No one really knew how it got there, nor did anyone know why it was called the Rumblerock. Today, on top of the Rumblerock, Yockenthwaite was holding a knitted sock stuffed full of grass over the opening of a drainpipe that had been nailed on to its side. At the bottom of the rock stood Roger, holding a stick in both hands . . .

'Now?' shouted Yockenthwaite.

'Three, two, one – drop!' Roger shouted back.

Yockenthwaite let go of the sock. Roger stood waiting at the bottom of the pipe. The sock came whizzing out. Roger tried to whack it. And missed . . .

'Bother!' (Roger didn't *actually* say 'bother', but that's what we had to put because you can't print words like 'rat's knickers' in books.) 'You can only trap it if you pick the *exact* moment it's going to come out.'

'What's this game called, King Roger?' asked Yockenthwaite.

'Rat up a Drainpipe,' said Roger.

'*Up* a drainpipe?' frowned Yockenthwaite.

'It's just a name,' said Roger.

'Yo-o!' hooted Yockenthwaite. 'Give us a bash!'

Roger had brought a spare bit of drainpipe from his stepdad's works and the moment he saw it, Yockenthwaite thought that 'Rat up a Drainpipe' was probably the *best* game he'd ever played in his whole life. But that's not surprising, because Yockenthwaite was totally rubbish at every other game he'd ever tried, and always came last. Here was one game, though, that he thought he might have a chance of being good at, which meant that when Roger explained that he had to go and help Penyghent collect some garlic, Yockenthwaite shrieked:

'Y'can't, I want to carry on practising.'

'Tomorrow, OK Yockenthwaite?' said Roger, walking away. 'Time to do some work.'

Now I'd *like* to say that at this point Yockenthwaite did what you'd do, that he'd be very grown up and think, 'That's fine. Tomorrow isn't too far off. I can wait.' Unfortunately, he didn't.

'*Baaaaaaaaaaaaaaaaaaaaaa!!!!*' he sobbed, whacking the ground with his stick. 'I want to carry on playing! *Baaaaaaaaaaaaaaaaaaaaa!!*'

'Ooooh!' said Blacksyke, who'd come to see what all the fuss was about. 'Sounds like you're upset, dearie.'

'I wanted to carry on playing,' whinged Yockenthwaite, 'but King Roger said he had to go and do some work . . .'

'Did he now,' smirked Blacksyke.

'Maybe he's right, though,' said Yockenthwaite.

'No!' Blacksyke shook her black-veiled head. 'He *should* stay, Yockenthwaite . . . if you asked him to, dearie . . .'

'D'you think?'

'No one takes you seriously, do they, dearie?' said Blacksyke, circling him slowly.

'No, they don't,' pouted Yockenthwaite. 'They all think I'm a berk.'

'If I was you, I wouldn't have it,' said Blacksyke slyly, 'I'd cause a bit of trouble, me . . . stir it up a bit . . . dig a bit of dirt . . . stick a bit of *brolly* in . . .'

And because Yockenthwaite really was a berk, that's exactly what he did.

'King Roger?' said Yockenthwaite, squirming in his seat. 'I . . . me . . . that is, myself . . . am,

like, fed up.'

'Pardon?' said Roger.

'No one takes me seriously. They think I'm a berk,' said Yockenthwaite. Everyone nodded in agreement. 'And no one does what I ask 'cos I always lose at games – and you didn't do what I asked yesterday up by the Rumblerock, and *you're* s'posed to be my friend and, and, and I *protest*!'

'You protest?' asked Roger, a bit puzzled by what was going on.

'Yes,' said Yockenthwaite, desperately trying to remember what Blacksyke had said he was to do. 'I'm, er, stirring up a bit of muddy and, er, dirtying me brolly . . . as a protest . . . King Roger.'

CHAPTER TEN

Now King Roger was only a 'King' by mistake, remember. He hadn't done any training, read any books, passed any exams and didn't have a GCSE in Kingliness (although he did have a Cubs badge for tying knots). But, like it or not, Yockenthwaite had a problem and, as King, Roger had to solve it – that was his job. So after a moment or two's thought (would you believe five minutes?) he had an idea. It wasn't a stonker, by any means, but it was better than no idea at all . . .

'I hereby announce,' said Roger, 'that I am abdicating as King of the Rottentrolls!'

Penyghent was shocked. 'You can't abdicate!' she said.

'What's abdicate?' asked Askrigg.

'It means 'to simmer gently in garlic sauce',' said Kettlewell. 'And I'll deck anyone who says it doesn't!'

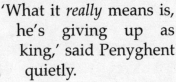

'What it *really* means is, he's giving up as king,' said Penyghent quietly.

'But why?' asked Aysgarth.

'Because I'm handing my throne to . . .' Roger turned and pointed, '. . . *Yockenthwaite!*'

'You can't do that!' spluttered Aysgarth. 'He's a berk – always has been, always will be!'

'Yo-o!' beamed Yockenthwaite. 'I'm King!'

'Well, go on,' said Roger, 'decree something then.'

'Oh . . . right . . . yeah, I know – I decree we all have to go and play 'Rat up a Drainpipe'!'

So they all did. And even though Yockenthwaite . . . sorry, *King* Yockenthwaite . . . was still rubbish at it and missed the rat every single time, things were different now . . .

'My go,' said Penyghent, when Yockenthwaite missed again.

'Hold on, I'm King,' said Yockenthwaite, 'and I decree that the King is allowed to keep whacking until he catches the rat!'

'Right,' said Aysgarth, some thirty minutes

of fruitless whacking later. 'I think it's time we did some work.'

'Nab Twins!' bellowed Kettlewell. 'I need some fresh garlic, sharpish!'

'No, no, NO!!' Yockenthwaite shouted. '*I* want to carry on playing.'

'We can't,' said Kettlewell.

'We can,' replied Yockenthwaite, 'I'm King, I decree it – no one is allowed to do any work. From now on, everyone just has to play games!'

So that's exactly what happened. Everyone had to play whatever game it was King Yockenthwaite wanted. First they played paper aeroplane races, to see whose plane went furthest. Of course Yockenthwaite, who tried to make his planes supersonic by folding them to death, always lost. Until, that is, he decreed Kings could carry theirs . . .

'Yo-o! Champion!'

When they played ping-pong across the ceremonial table (that was once a door) in the Great Cave, Yockenthwaite won because he decreed the King was allowed a bigger bat – at a very rough guess, one about the size of an elephant's underpants . . .

'Yo-o! Champion!'

Ping-pong was followed by Hide and Seek, where Yockenthwaite won again because he decreed no one was allowed to hide behind anything bigger than a small cushion . . .

'I am the winner! I am ace!'

Eventually, Yockenthwaite was too breathless with excitement to play anything else, so he tried to think of what it was he liked best *after* playing games and he had what *he* thought was a bright idea. About as bright as a dud 40 watt bulb, if you ask me . . .

'That's it – a party!' he grinned. 'I decree we all have a party – bring in the garlic pasties and the blueberry champagne!'

Everyone just stood and looked at him.

'Go on,' said Yockenthwaite, 'I decree it – chop-chop!'

'There isn't any blueberry champagne, King Yockenthwaite,' said Penyghent, 'because you didn't let us pick any blueberries.'

'But . . .'

'And what's more,' she carried on, 'I don't want to be at a party given by someone I don't like any more!'

'Yeah, dude!' huffed Great Nab. 'Yer like "Mr I-Have-To-Win-All-The-Time"!'

'Totally non-radical,' muttered Small Nab. 'Party on yer own, dude.'

'Come back!' ordered Yockenthwaite, as

everyone trailed out of the Great Cave. 'Everyone sit down – I decree it!'

And moments later, the only person left in the cave was a very small, very quiet, very alone little Yockenthwaite . . .

'But . . . but . . . I *decreed* it . . .' said Yockenthwaite sadly. 'I've decreed. Didn't anyone hear me just then? Decreeing?'

Actually, not everyone had left the cave.

'You all right, King Yockenthwaite?' asked Roger.

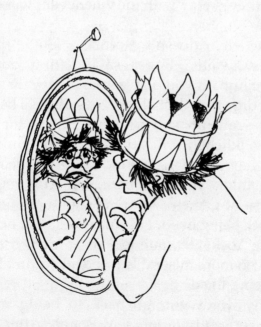

'No.'

'Great being King, in't it?'

'No,' sulked Yockenthwaite. 'It's *rubbish*, I hate it!'

'Really, why?'

Yockenthwaite squirmed on the throne. 'Y'don't have any friends . . .'

'I don't think that's true,' said Roger.

'Well I haven't, not now.'

'Why did you think it would be any better if you were king?' asked Roger.

'Because I thought they wouldn't treat me like a berk any more,' replied Yockenthwaite. 'And they'd play with me whenever I wanted to.'

'But it doesn't work like that, Yockenthwaite,' Roger said, sitting down next to him. 'If you play games all day there'll be no time to collect blueberries, there'll be no garlic – all fun and no work makes for an empty kitchen.' Roger, surprised himself with how wise he sounded. 'And people don't think you're a berk just 'cos you're rubbish at games – winning's got nothing to do with being liked. I mean, look at you now.'

King Yockenthwaite looked at himself and got even more miserable. He really didn't like not being liked.

'Why don't you go back to being non-King Yockenthwaite?' said Roger. 'After all,

that's the person everyone liked in the first place!'

Now, even though Roger had precisely no qualifications for being a King, he'd managed to come up with a pretty smart solution. Well done, Roger. And Yockenthwaite thought it was a very 'Yo-o!' sort of idea as well and gleefully resigned his throne (by chucking the crown in a corner of the Great Cave) and ran off up the valley.

He did a lot of hithering and thithering, collecting pocketfuls of blueberries, bunches of nettles, a few bits of parsley and quite a lot of some strange green stuff that he knew nothing about, but thought it looked pretty tasty. Anyway, then he went back to his cave and mashed the whole lot up, which he really enjoyed 'cos it was messy, and *then* he mixed that lot up with a load of fizzy water from the waterfall to make . . .

'Yockenthwaite's Special Blueberry, Nettle and Something Champagne!'

Right . . . scrummy, I suppose, if you like that kind of thing.

At which point it was tea-time and, as soon as everyone had arrived in the Great Cave, Yockenthwaite began pouring his blue brew into glasses.

'Rottentrolls and Trollslips!' he said. 'I'd like to make another decree – and that is, I'm not King any more!'

'All, like, right!' said Great Nab.

'Yeah, cool, dude!' agreed Small Nab.

'I'm giving the crown back to King Roger,' Yockenthwaite went on, 'and I'd also like to say . . . er . . . sorry for anything I've done during my, like, kingship. So, to make up for anything I *did* do, I've made you all some of my Special Blueberry, Nettle and Something Champagne!'

There were huge cheers all round, because everyone really was very glad to have the normal Yockenthwaite back. Then everyone took a swig of the normal Yockenthwaite's special champagne, which kind of spoilt the moment as they all had to spit it out again because the normal Yockenthwaite was a complete berk and couldn't guess his own name, let alone make a decent drink . . .

'Yo-o!' said Yockenthwaite. 'That green stuff's not bad, is it?'

CHAPTER ELEVEN

Since his arrival in Troller's Ghyll, Roger had met some serious nutcases, but the real fruitiest fruit-and-nut-case of the lot was Sigsworthy Crags, the maddest of the Rottentrolls by a long chalk. If you asked the other Rottentrolls about him they'd say things like, 'He's a blithering idiot!' or, 'Well weird, man!' or, 'He's completely nuts!'

Coming from Yockenthwaite, this was really saying something, and if you asked King Roger he'd say, 'Sigsworthy Crags? He's mad. He's got stupid hair, he makes a noise like a dog and keeps going on about this airship he's built which everyone knows he hasn't, 'cos he's totally *mad*!'

See? The man could win Gold for his country in the Bonkers Olympics. So you can imagine the surprise when Sigsworthy Crags burst through the undergrowth next to Roger,

Aysgarth and Penyghent and shouted, 'I've finished me airship! It's built! And you're the King, so you've got to launch it!'

Of course, at that point, what nobody knew was that Sigsworthy Crags had been collecting every helium balloon that had ever floated over Troller's Ghyll, trying to get enough of them to lift an old council bin off the ground. So they just followed him, thinking that he really must've flipped this time.

'Morning, Commander Harris,' said Roger as they passed the leader of the Troller's

Ghyll SAS. 'Fancy coming up to Sigsworthy's cave – he *says* he's finished his airship!'

'No can do, King Roger,' said the Commander. 'Waiting for the delivery of me new radar dish, y'see.'

'I thought you already had one on your roof?'

'True, very true, but that old thing only picks up sheep in *this* valley,' explained the Commander. 'The new one can put me in touch with sheep movements across Northern Europe!'

'OK, no probs,' said Roger. 'You won't be missing anything 'cos Sigsworthy's just going to start barking again – I don't even know why I'm bothering . . .'

Roger said this as he walked over the rise and looked down at Sigsworthy Crags' cave.

'Wow!'

Wow indeed. Not only had good old Sigsworthy got a cracking collection of *ordinary*-sized helium balloons in various bright colours (which were fairly impressive in their own right) but yesterday he'd been lucky enough to discover the very thing he needed to lift his old council bin off the ground. It was a huge, green, sprout-shaped helium balloon that had detached itself from the Sprout Advisory Council's stand at the Cowgill Agricultural Show. It was green, and it had *'EAT MORE SPROUTS!'* written on it.

'You all thought I was nuts, didn't you!' crowed Sigsworthy, stroking his balloons.

'Er . . . yes,' said everyone who'd gathered to watch.

'Well *thrrrrp*!! to the lot of you!' said Sigsworthy, climbing into the old council bin. 'Because, I, Sigsworthy Crags, am about to become the furthest travelled of all Rottentrolls, ever!'

'Don't be ridiculous!' said Aysgarth. 'Get out of that thing – where d'you think you're going?'

'The African jungle!'

'You'll never get that far, man,' said Great Nab.

'Right on, bro,' agreed Small Nab. 'Africa is, like, *miles* away, dude!'

'I know that. D'you think I'm stupid?' said Sigsworthy, untying the anchoring ropes. 'It's on the other side of the world and I'm about to go there – farewell Troller's Ghyll! Farewell Rottentrolls! One, two, three *LIFT OFF!!'*

Having got over the shock of seeing something that looked fairly like an airship, the general opinion was that it would fly about as well as the Rumblerock. But they were wrong, and to everyone's great surprise the balloon did what they'd least expected it to do. It rose into the air.

'The Eagle has taken off!' yelled Sigsworthy, as the balloon started to go higher and higher. 'This is one small step for a Rottentroll ... one great leap for a kangaroo – A-*rooo! A-roooo-ooo!!*'

'He's nuts,' said Great Nab. 'Like totally Brazil, man.'

'I heard that!' yelled Sigsworthy. 'You'll see if I don't do it – you'll see!'

'You know what I think?' said Yockenthwaite. '*I* think he might make it to the African jungle.'

CHAPTER TWELVE

The fact that Yockenthwaite thought Sigsworthy Crags could fly to Africa in an old council bin with a bunch of helium balloons tied to it, (even if one of them was a huge green sprout), wasn't really a worry. The worry was that he was flying at all.

'What d'you think, Penyghent?' said Roger.

'I think we'd better go after him.'

'That's what I think, too . . .'

So they all ran to the top of the rocks.

'Can you see him?' asked Roger.

'Nope,' said Yockenthwaite, who was actually looking at an ants' nest.

'He could be anywhere!' said Roger worriedly.

'No he couldn't,' Penyghent shook her head. 'They're only balloons, they can only go in the direction the wind blows.'

'How do we know which way he went

then?' asked Yockenthwaite.

'Give me a straw,' said Penyghent, showing that she wasn't just a pretty face who knew the names of eight different kinds of fish. Grabbing the straw that Yockenthwaite was chewing, she threw it in the air.

'That was me favourite!' protested Yockenthwaite.

'He went *that* way,' Penyghent pointed the way the straw had gone.

'Uh-oh . . .' said Roger.

Up in the sky, in the direction Penyghent had pointed, floated the reason Roger went 'Uh-oh'. It was a pink balloon, and looked suspiciously like a pink balloon that a few moments ago had been attached to Sigsworthy Crags' old council bin.

'That looks like one of Sigsworthy's,' said Roger.

'And so does that ... and that ...' said Penyghent.

'His balloons must be coming loose,' said Roger. 'Correct me if I'm wrong, Penyghent, but if *adding* balloons means Sigsworthy went *up* ...'

'Taking them *away*,' she went on, 'means he must go ...'

'Swimming?' asked Yockenthwaite.

'No - down!' Roger and Penyghent shouted at the same time.

How right they both were. As the balloons came undone (Sigsworthy Crags lacking that all-important Cubs badge in knot tying, so necessary when attempting a balloon flight to Africa), the dustbin did a very good impression of the Rumblerock and plummeted to the ground.

'All your balloons came undone!' said Penyghent, when they got to where Sigsworthy had landed.

'Except the giant floating sprout,' said Yockenthwaite.

'Yes, well ... I never was that good at knots,' said Sigsworthy, getting up. 'Still, here I am – the African jungle! The other side of the world!'

'It's not the other side of the world,' said Roger.

'Course it is ... it must be!' Sigsworthy looked around. 'I've never seen it before and I know what *our* side looks like!'

'The world's a big place, Sigsworthy. Round, like this balloon,' Roger patted the giant sprout. 'You've not gone that far.'

'What? Y'r nuts!' said Sigsworthy. 'The world's flat, with a bit of jam in the top right hand corner – everyone knows that!'

'That's just your map,' said Penyghent.

'And *this* is just the other side of the moor,' said Roger.

'Rubbish!' scowled Sigsworthy. 'Load of old codswallop – if this is still our side of the world, how come we don't know anyone, eh?'

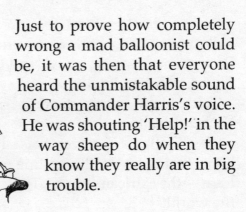

Just to prove how completely wrong a mad balloonist could be, it was then that everyone heard the unmistakable sound of Commander Harris's voice. He was shouting 'Help!' in the way sheep do when they know they really are in big trouble.

'Commander Harris!' yelled Roger, rushing towards his shed. 'What are you doing?'

'Roger, King Roger ... it's me new radar antenna,' explained the Commander. 'It turned out slightly bigger than I was expecting.'

'Are you *supposed* to climb right to the top of it?' enquired Roger, peering up at the extraordinary sight of a sheep in a Balaclava helmet hanging on for dear life to a rather rickety tangle of metal rods.

'Not according to the instructional manual
. . . no,' said the Commander. 'But something
went wrong with the tuning, and, instead of
picking up sheep movements in Northern
Europe, it was getting *cow* movements in
South America. I came up here to adjust it,
and then I looked down.'

'Are you all right?' asked Roger.

'To be perfectly honest, King Roger, I am
not,' replied the Commander. 'I'm awfully
sorry, but I'm going to have to cry –
BAAAAAAAAAAA!!'

'Don't panic, Commander,' said Roger,
'Sigsworthy, give us y'r sprout!'

Sigsworthy looked horrified. He'd worked
extremely hard to collect all those lovely
helium balloons, and now someone
wanted him to hand over the only one he
had left.

'It's me last one!' complained Sigsworthy.

'But the Commander's trapped!' said
Roger.

'What about me trip back from the African
jungle?'

'*BAAAAAAAAAAA!!!*'

'*Sigsworthy!!*'

'Oh . . . all right . . .'

Sigsworthy Crags did the decent thing and

handed over his giant green floating sprout to King Roger.

'Commander Harris,' said Roger, 'are you ready to catch this when it gets up to you?'

'I should cocoa!'

'What's the plan, King Roger?' asked Penyghent.

'Remember what happened to Sigsworthy when *he* only had this balloon left?'

'He was too heavy and came back down to earth,' said Penyghent.

'Well ditto Commander Harris when he catches hold of the sprout!'

'Brilliant!' said Penyghent.

'OK,' said Roger, 'jump when I tell you to.'

'Jump?' spluttered the Commander. 'Are you mad, sir?'

'I know sheep don't normally do this, Commander,' said Roger, letting go of the sprout, 'but sheep don't normally get stuck up a radar antenna – three . . . two . . . one . . . *JUMP!!*'

The Commander yelled 'Karamba!' and leapt for the balloon. But instead of grabbing the string he actually landed on it, fell to the ground and burst the best chance the Sprout Advisory Council had had for years of getting people to eat more greens.

'My word!' said the Commander when he realised he was on solid ground once more.

'My hero!' said Penyghent, gazing adoringly at her King.

'My sprout!' wailed Sigsworthy. He picked up the deflated canvas. For all the world it looked like a . . . like a . . . like a huge burst sprout. 'They'll all say I'm nuts now . . . they'll all say "We knew he'd never get to the African jungle – we knew his airship wouldn't work!" . . . but it *did* work, didn't it? Until it stopped working . . .'

'Jungle?' said Commander Harris, pricking up his ears. 'Does someone want to know what the African jungle's like?'

Commander Harris, who, for a sheep, was a bit of a squirrel, had kept a lot of souvenirs of his time in the Army, and from an old chest in his command hut he took out a photograph . . .

'Took this on me last day as mascot to the Royal Fusiliers,' he said, handing the picture over to Sigsworthy.

'I never knew you'd been in the jungle,' said Sigsworthy.

'Where else d'you think I learnt the ancient martial art of Jimjam YaHA!?'

For some odd reason we'll never know, this was when King Roger had a brilliant idea . . . well, brilliant for a bloke who quite enjoyed being the king of a bunch of mad trolls.

'Commander Harris . . . you know how, by helping to rescue you, Sigsworthy here had to give up something that was very dear to him?' said Roger.

'Roger, King Roger,' nodded the Commander.

'Well d'you think you might, sort of, like help *him* out now by giving him something that was dear to you?'

'Like what, sir?'

Word soon got round Troller's Ghyll about Sigsworthy Crags' great adventure, mainly because it was the only interesting thing to have happened since the last interesting thing, and no one could remember what that was.

'And this,' said Sigsworthy, handing the photo to Aysgarth, 'is the very photographic picture of the African jungle I took from out of me airship when I was gliding over it!'

'Don't be so ridiculous!' scoffed Aysgarth. 'You never went to Africa . . . let me have a good look at that.'

'You're just jealous 'cos I'm now the furthest travelled Rottentroll ever!'

'I most certainly am not jealous!' said Aysgarth jealously, looking round the Great Cave for some support, and finding none. 'I know who'll tell us if it's true or not – King Roger, is Sigsworthy Crags telling the truth, or is he, as we've always suspected, a total nut case?'

Problem. Big problem. Roger knew that a King couldn't lie, and he also knew that Sigsworthy *hadn't* really been to Africa. So he thought a bit, and then he said, 'That, Aysgarth, is definitely a photo of the African jungle.'

Which, after all, was the truth.

'Thanks, King Roger!' said Sigsworthy.

'I'm your King,' smiled Roger, patting Sigsworthy on the back. 'Any time I can help, just let me know.'

'Really? That's great!' said Sigsworthy. 'Cos next week I'm building a rocket!'

CHAPTER THIRTEEN

The weather had taken a dip in Troller's Ghyll. All yesterday was really sunny and the hidden valley had been baking hot, but now the sky was grey and all the rocks had gone cool. By which I mean they'd gone cold, rather than they'd started hanging round outside record shops in large white trainers and T-shirts with logos all over them.

Anyway, Yockenthwaite was playing a game he'd made up called 'See How Many Stones You Can Fit In Your Pockets Before You Trip Over And Hurt Yourself', and Penyghent was amusing herself by following behind him saying 'Don't fill your pockets with stones, 'cos you'll trip over and hurt yourself'. They both stopped what they were doing when they saw King Roger sitting all alone on a rock, looking pretty miserable.

'He doesn't usually come into the valley without telling us,' said Yockenthwaite.

'What's the matter, King Roger?' asked Penyghent.

'Nothing . . . just leave me alone, thanks,' muttered Roger.

'But we're your oldest friends,' said Yockenthwaite.

Which, if you didn't count the thirty or so mates Roger had been in the same class with since primary school, was perfectly true.

'You've always helped us if we're in trouble,' said Penyghent, sitting next to him, 'and we're here to help if *you* are.'

'I'm not,' said Roger, looking away. 'I've just run away from home, that's all. I'm coming here to live . . . I've brought me favourite lamp.'

'We don't have electricity,' said Yockenthwaite.

'I know, but . . . but I've brought it anyway,' sighed Roger. 'And some food and pyjamas . . . I'll find a cave . . .'

'You can't live in Troller's Ghyll!' said Penyghent.

'Why not? OK, so it's full of mad trolls, but I'll get used to it.'

'Your parent's'll be worried,' said Yockenthwaite. 'Your mum and stepdad.'

'Yeah, well . . .' Roger chucked a stone at another stone, 'they shouldn't treat me like a kid then, should they? They shouldn't make me go to bed at eight o'clock like a kid – they don't realise I'm a *King*! And if I'm old enough to be a King, I'm old enough to stay up as late as me mates do. If they don't like it, they can just lump it . . . I'm staying here and never going back!'

Before Yockenthwaite and Penyghent had a chance to reply, the valley was filled with an unearthly howl, and it wasn't Sigsworthy Crags going all Battersea Dogs' Home again. It was, unmistakably, Kettlewell . . .

'*AAARGHHHH!!!*'

'What's the matter, Kettlewell?' asked Roger, pelting into the cave.

'It's Strid, me baby Trollslip . . . she went wandering off!' sobbed Kettlewell.

'Askrigg said he saw her heading towards the deserted lead mine at the valley top,' said Aysgarth, doing his best (but failing) to comfort Kettlewell. 'That's where the entrance to the Barguest's cave is.'

'The Barguest . . .' said Roger, very slowly. 'Him with the big red eyes . . .'

'That's right, the huge horse-y dog with eyes as big as dinner plates,' nodded Aysgarth. 'What're you going to do, King Roger?'

'Me?' said Roger, suddenly remembering that he'd so recently said something very like, 'I'm y'r King, any time I can help, just let me know,' and really wishing he hadn't.

'Right everyone,' said Aysgarth. 'King Roger will now reveal his Great Plan to rescue little Strid from the lead mines!'

Roger looked at all the expectant faces.

'King Roger,' Yockenthwaite tugged at his sleeve, 'if you can't plug it in, d'you still want that lamp?'

'Quiet, Yockenthwaite,' said Aysgarth.

Just then, Roger noticed something in the corner of the cave. It was a load of string left over from making the Extraordinary Dinner Telephone, and for some reason it looked sort of *useful*; but how could it help him go down a lead mine and rescue little Strid from a socking great monster? He was just going to give up when he had one of those terrific light bulb moments.

'Brilliant!' grinned Roger, as the story they'd done in History at school last Wednesday started to come back to him . . .

Last Wednesday, Roger had learnt all about the Minotaur, a mythical Greek monster that was half man and half bull. This character was so narked about being kept in an underground maze that he ate anyone who got lost there. Some Greek hero had gone into the maze, killed the Minotaur and got out again because he'd left a trail of – you've guessed it ... string – to find his way back. Pretty nifty idea, if you think about it.

Anyway, Roger remembered the lesson, which was lucky really because this wasn't always the case, and told the Rottentrolls all about it.

'In the story, did the hero have a sword?' asked Penyghent when he'd finished.

'Yes,' said Roger.

'What've you got?'

'A Ryan Giggs table lamp,' sighed Roger.

'Can I have it?' Yockenthwaite asked again.

'But I know who *might* have a sword!' said Roger, ignoring Yockenthwaite, as usual.

'Sword?' said Commander Harris, leaning back against the wall of his command hut. 'Not me – you don't need swords when you're a Black Belt in Jimjam YaHA!'

'But how am I going to scare off the Barguest, Commander?'

'Lost me there, King Roger,' said the Commander. 'The only thing I've got that's vaguely to do with dogs is a tin of ceremonial dog food ... presented to me by the Commanding Officer of the King's Regiment in Hong Kong. Chap thought I'd be an alsatian; bit embarrassing really.'

'Must've been,' agreed Roger, who then had his *second* bright idea of the day. 'Are you ever going to eat it?'

'Hardly, old son,' sniffed the Commander. 'It's lamb flavour ...'

Roger now had to get a bit of a move on as it wouldn't be long before it was dark, and he didn't have a torch.

'Right,' he said, 'almost ready – I've got string, dog food ... all I need now is a torch.'

'That's easy,' said Yockenthwaite, 'use the one on y'r bike!'

'It doesn't come off,' said Roger.

'You mean "didn't",' laughed Yockenthwaite, handing it to him.

'Thank you *so* much ...' Roger grabbed the mangled torch. 'OK, I'm now ready to go and rescue Strid. Synchronise watches everyone.'

'We don't have any, King Roger,' apologised Aysgarth.

'No. Right. Never mind . . . just keep your fingers crossed.'

Roger went off up the valley and turned right into the deserted, abandoned, derelict, neglected, vacant – you get the general idea – the lead mine was, on the whole, somewhere he'd rather not be.

So he stood there (thinking quite a lot about being just about anywhere else) not making any noise. He was quiet, everything was quiet. Really quite quiet. Which was why he nearly lost it completely when a voice behind him said, 'Roger?'

'*AAAARGHHH!!!*' went Roger, his scream echoing back to him from deep within the tunnel. 'What are you playing at, Penyghent? It's very dangerous, y'know, I'm being very brave, doing this.'

'Yockenthwaite and I used to come up here all the time, for dares,' said Penyghent. 'The Barguest lives down there in a huge nest of fire.'

'*REALLY*?' squeaked Roger.

'Really . . . really . . . really?' his echo replied.

'Oh, why did I have to be King?' whispered Roger. 'Why couldn't I have been Minister for Sport, or something?'

'Pardon?'

'Nothing, Penyghent – just do me a favour, eh? Keep hold of this string and *don't* let go!'

'Good luck, King Roger,' said Penyghent.

And with that, Roger went underground . . .

CHAPTER FOURTEEN

Down in the tunnel, the stones were like fish. By which I mean they were cold and slimy, rather than fried, and surrounded by chips. Anyway, somewhere far away Roger could hear a ghastly, rib-shredding, gut-ripping, turn-your-blood-to-cold-porridge sort of noise . . .

'Right. That's it. I'll try again tomorrow.'

And then he heard someone go . . .

'*HEEEEELP!!*'

It could only have been Strid. He knew he had no choice but to carry on. So he did. Everywhere he looked he saw horrible faces (some of which seemed not unlike his teachers) in the shadowy tunnel walls, every twist and turn of which took him closer and closer to the bottomless pit-type noises. Soon the light and the heat were getting so strong he thought that the huge fire nest must be

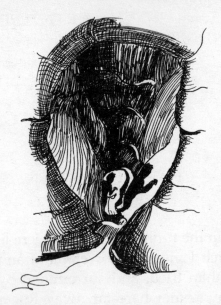

round the next corner. And, though he *really* didn't want to be, he was right . . .

'This is it, Barguest here I come . . .' he said to himself, coming out into a massive flame-filled cave that made the Great Cave look like a cubby-hole. 'Now *that's* what I call a big fire.' He squinted into the glare. 'Strid, are you there?'

'Help! Help!'

'Don't worry,' he said, spotting her clinging to a rock inches from the flaming pit, 'It's King Roger here – I've come to save you from the . . .'

'BARGUEST?' said a hot, brain-shrivelingly

scary voice. 'WHO HAS ENTERED THE FIRE NEST OF THE BARGUEST?'

'Er . . . me,' said Roger. 'Roger Becket. From Cowgill . . . Hugh Gaitskell Crescent . . . you know, near the Co-op. Have you ever been to Cowgill?'

'*R-ROOOOOAR!!*'

'No? Well you should,' said Roger, a pale grin pasted on his face. 'It won the Best Kept Village Award in 1983 . . . no, sorry, 1984 . . .'

'YOU WILL BE *EATEN*!' growled the Barguest.

'Right, now look . . . the thing is . . . like . . . you know . . .' Roger's throat felt drier than a whole packet of Cream Crackers when he tried to swallow.

'Truth is, I taste *horrible*! Honest – really bony,' said Roger, who suddenly remembered what he was carrying with him. 'But have you tried new lamb-flavoured *WuffChunks*?' he yelled, lobbing the can right into the Barguest's open mouth. 'Sink your fangs into that!' Which the Barguest duly did.

'AARGH!' it roared. 'GNY GEETH ARE STUGG!!'

For a split second, maybe just a *little* bit longer, the mighty jaws of the Barguest were about as useful as a bath without a plug – stuck, as they were, in Commander Harris's

tin of ceremonial dog food. And that split second was all Roger needed.

'Hang on, Strid!' yelled Roger, grabbing the little Trollslip while the going was good, which it was for a moment or two, until Roger realised that he couldn't find the string that would lead them back out of the tunnel.

'Where's it gone?' squeaked Roger, as he searched frantically for what had once been part of the Great (Failed) Troller's Ghyll Telephone Experiment ... and finally found it. 'Got you!'

'COME BACK AND BE EATEN!' The Barguest had disentangled its teeth from the tin of *WuffChunks* and was still hungry. Roger, with Strid hanging on to his back, pelted off down the tunnel like the clappers.

He went left!

He went right!

The Barguest did the same.

He went faster!

The Barguest went faster still.

Oh good lord . . . the tension's killing me, it's just like *James Bond*, only without the tailored suits and ejector seats and Miss Moneypenny. In fact it's nothing like *James Bond* at all, more along the lines of *The Bill*, except there weren't any sirens and uniforms, and not much sign of police cars, truncheons and whistles either. In fact it was nothing like *The Bill*, either, it was just one young chap, with a small Rottentroll clinging to his back for dear life, being chased by a fairly rabid monster (with eyes as big as dinner plates) who was trying to dislodge a tin of lamb-flavoured dog food from his teeth so he could get something slightly more tasty down his throat. Oh, the every-day life of country folk . . . doesn't it make living in suburbia seem rather boring?

So on and on ran Roger, pelting as fast as he could and wishing that he hadn't skipped quite so many gym lessons – up passages, down passages, round bends and down what began to look exactly like the passage they'd just been up. Then he spotted something . . .

'OK, Strid,' panted Roger, 'either this next little tunnel's a short cut ... or *we're* dog food!'

'Weeee-eee!' said Strid, (who, for some odd reason, hadn't clicked she was the starter on the Barguest's menu, and was having a really terrific time).

'RR-R-R-RAAATS!!' roared the Barguest, turning the corner in time to see his first and second courses just managed to get away ...

'Look,' yelled Yockenthwaite, who was staring down the tunnel. 'He's here – King Roger's here, and he's got Strid!'

'Made it!' said Roger, emerging breathless, mud-splattered and sooty from the dark chasm and handing Strid over to Kettlewell.

'Can I have y'r lamp?' whispered Yockenthwaite.

CHAPTER FIFTEEN

That night, there was a big party in Troller's Ghyll. Kettlewell was so happy to have little Strid back in one piece she even tried to make honey flapjacks. Nice going, Kettlewell, but next time try to remember to put the honey in.

Anyway, there was plenty of blueberry champagne, everyone sang the National Anthem and Trucklecrag magicked up some fireworks. Which was a shame, since he was actually trying for some cheeseburgers and fizzy-pop to get rid of the taste of the honey-less flapjacks.

'Oh pig . . .'

And then, at the end of the evening, Roger announced he was going home.

'Home? We thought you'd run away from home,' said Penyghent.

'You mean y'r *not* going to live in the valley?' said Yockenthwaite.

'Maybe another time,' smiled Roger, picking up his things. 'I'll see you later . . .'

'Bye, King Roger!' said all the Rottentrolls, waving as he left.

'D'you think we helped him, Penyghent?' asked Yockenthwaite when he'd gone.

'I don't know, Yockenthwaite,' she said sadly. 'He helps us, but I doubt we can help him . . . he's a King.'

'What, like Elvis?'

Distantly over Troller's Ghyll there echoed the sound of a small bobble-hatted head being whacked by one of Kettlewell's bigger frying pans.

So there it is. THE END, sort of . . . story over, lessons learned.

'What lessons?' do I hear you ask? Oh, I don't know . . . ones like the fact that running away from home isn't such a great idea, because, even though you've rowed with your Mum and stepdad, you wouldn't want *them* to go through all that panic the Rottentrolls went through over little Strid.

And what have *I* learned?

Ahem.

Jimjam YaHA!

I think I can say with some confidence that someone somewhere has just gone flying off their bike. If it was you, I'm sorry abut that, but then again you shouldn't have been reading a book while you were cycling.

Hving said that, of course, thanks for buying the book in the first place, obviously. So in a sense the last thing I'd like to say is the same as the first thing I said. And now that I've started to repeat myself it's probably time to go.

Goodbye.

Or, as they say in Troller's Ghyll ... 'Goodbye'.

The End.
(Really).

Troller's Ghyll valley is the secret home of The 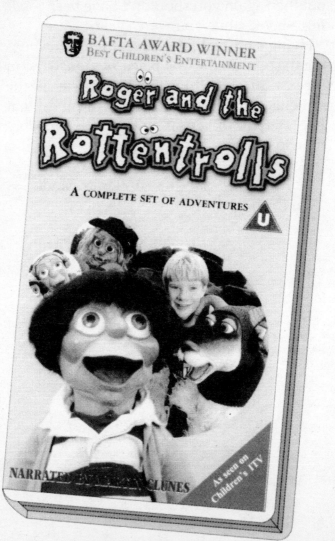, a bunch of crazy, knee-high characters who were dropped from the sky in Merlin the Magician's snowcloud experiment. When 10 ¾ year old Roger Becket crashes his bike into the valley, he doesn't suspect that he is about to be crowned King of the Rottentrolls and set out on a series of amazing adventures.

Now you can join Roger and his Troll friends in this zany video collection which contains all the episodes from Series 1 of **ITV's BAFTA** Award winning TV series.

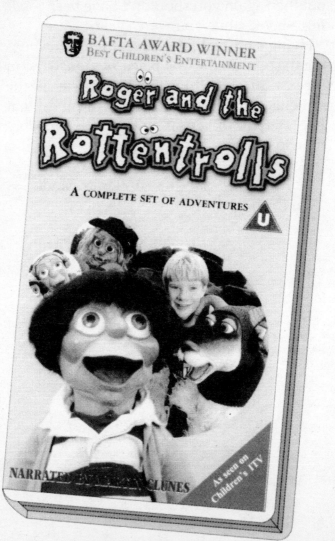

Available to buy from all good video stockists from 6th April 19
Catalogue No: Vc1491, RRP: £9.99